Mad IN THE Back

For Emma, Elsie and Emile – M.R.

For my parents, and all the times my brother and I went mad in the back! – R.W.

Published in 2021 in Great Britain by
Barrington Stoke Ltd
18 Walker Street, Edinburgh, EH3 7LP

www.barringtonstoke.co.uk

This edition based on *Mad in the Back*
(Barrington Stoke, 2015)

This story was first published in a different form in
The Hypnotiser (André Deutsch, 1988)

Text © 1988 & 2021 Michael Rosen
Illustrations © 2015 Richard Watson

A CIP catalogue record for this book is available
from the British Library upon request

ISBN: 978-1-80090-078-3

Printed by Hussar Books, Poland

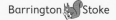

Barrington Stoke

Mad IN THE Back

Michael Rosen

Illustrated by
Richard Watson

Mum says, "Right, you two, this is a very long car journey. I want you two to be good. I'm driving and I can't drive safely if you two are going mad in the back."

So we say, "OK, Mum, OK. Don't worry."

And off we go.

And we start The Moaning.

"Can I have a drink?"

"I want some crisps."

"Can I open my window?"

4

"He's got my book."

"Get off me."

"Ow, that's my ear!"

And Mum tries to make us stop. "Look out the window – there's a lamp-post."

9

And we go on with The Moaning.

"Can I have a sweet?"

"He's sitting on me."

"Are we nearly there?"

"Don't scratch."

"You never tell him off."

"Now he's biting his nails."

"I want a drink."

"I want a drink."

13

And Mum tries again to make us stop.

"Look out the window – there's a tree."

And we go on.

"My hands are sticky."

"He's playing with the door handle now."

"I feel sick."

"Your nose is all runny."

"Don't pull my hair."

"He's punching me, Mum. Mum, he's spitting."

And Mum says, "Right, I'm stopping the car.
I AM STOPPING THE CAR."

She stops the car.

"Now, if you two don't stop it I'm going to put you out of the car and leave you by the side of the road."

"She started it."

"I didn't. He started it."

"I don't care who started it. I can't drive properly if you two go mad in the back. Do you understand?"

And we say, "OK, Mum, OK, don't worry."

25

HAVE YOU READ THEM ALL?

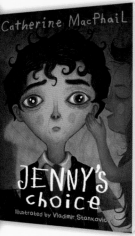

Cornelia Funke

Gawain Greytail and the Terrible Tab

Illustrated by Monica Armino

MOLLY ROGERS PIRATE GIRL

Cornelia Funke

Illustrated by Kasia Matyjaszek

ALEXANDER McCALL SMITH

BOING BOING

ILLUSTRATED BY ZOE PERSICO

Michael Rosen

Illustrated by Richard Watson

Mad in the Back

MICHAEL ROSEN

Wolfman

Illustrated by Chris Mould

ELEANOR UPDALE

Illustrated by Sarah Horne

Itch Scritch Scratch

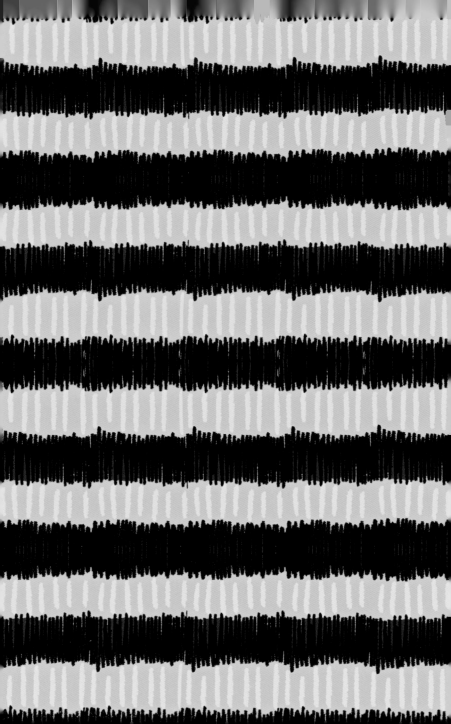